THE ADVENTUROUS LIFE
of a CAPE COD DOG

The Adventurous Life of a Cape Cod Dog

A Curious Canine's Exploration of the Cape's Natural History

by Nancy Scaglione-Peck

Illustrations by Jenny Kelley

Outer Cape Escape Publishing

Outer Cape Escape Publishing

ISBN 978-0-9914339-0-2

To sit with a dog on a hillside on a glorious afternoon is to be back in Eden, where doing nothing was not boring - it was peace.
~Milan Kundera

For Shelby

The Early Years

It is getting to be that time of year again. It's warming up. The days are longer and the Cape Cod spring fog is finally lifting. My parents are home a lot more. Nancy, my Mom, is readying the house for our guests, and my Dad, Bob, is constantly working in the yard. They are busy but happy. They are teachers, and school is almost done for the summer. This is my favorite time of year. It means more quality time, more trips to the donut shop, more walks on the beach, and more boat rides. It means whale watches, camping in the dunes, and day trips to all the tourist areas of Cape Cod—and lots of attention from our bed & breakfast guests. That usually means lots of snacks.

I'm Shelby a Golden-Chow mix canine and host of the Outer Cape Escape Bed & Breakfast. This is my story. It's my adventurous life as a Cape Cod dog!

Life for me started out pretty typically for a dog. My biological mom was a Golden Retriever and, from what I have been told, my biological dad was a Chow, but I am not sure of that because I have never met him. I had many siblings that I have some memories of, but not many. What I remember most about my brothers and sisters is how we all snuggled against our mom to eat and stay warm. I still remember the sweet smell and taste of her warm milk and her soft fur. I felt comforted by her warm breath on my cool nose and paws. I know she loved me close to her because, as I grew and began to explore, she would always catch me in her mouth and carry me back to our pack.

Little by little our pack got smaller as nice people came to visit us. I was the last to leave my mom, so I know I was very special and we shared a special bond. For a short time, I lived with a very nice woman. We spent a lot of time together, and I learned I could make her happy if did things like sit and stay when she asked. She took me to the beach a lot. I loved the beach for all its wonderful smells and open space. I could run and run forever. For some reason when I was younger, I loved to eat shells. I remember getting scolded for that because the woman said eating them was bad for my teeth! But for me it was fun because they always smelled good and tasted pretty good, too. Other than that, I don't remember too much of my first year of life.

My most vivid memories began the day I met my real dad at the pound. It was a noisy place with lots of barking dogs and screeching cats. It wasn't a place I wanted to be, but I remember the people there were real nice. As I rested in my cage, a nice man stopped by and looked at the sign on my cage and said, "Shelby, aren't you a handsome boy!" He knelt down, looked into my eyes and said, "Smart, too!" And I remember thinking, "Well, so are you!" After all, he was right. I am smart *and* good looking! He let himself in my cage and sat with me for a while. He petted me in all the right places and talked nicely to me. He even took me for a walk. I remember thinking how much I liked his smell. Eventually, he left and I remember feeling a little sad. It reminded me of how I missed my biological mom at times. Feeling this way told me he must be a special man. The next day, he returned. Again, he sat with me and took me for a walk. This time, we played ball together. It was fun because he could throw the ball really far so I could run farther and faster. The next day he didn't return but a nice young lady stood by my cage and said my name. She entered my cage and I immediately jumped up on her. This made her giggle and she kissed my muzzle. It was as if I had known her, although we had never met before. But I recognized her smell. She smelled just like that nice man who had visited me. Shortly after, he came in! They put me on a leash, and I walked out of that pound one last time. We jumped in their truck and we went to the beach. We walked and ran and played. They told me to stop eating the shells and pulled them out of my mouth. Mom wondered if my love for shells is what got me the name Shelby. They wondered who would have ever given me up to the pound and why, but were thankful that person had. And so was I. Already, I could feel their love for me, and our mutual love of the beach is a special bond we've always shared. We were an instant Cape Cod family!

Shelby Goes on a Whale Watch

Cape Cod is a special place. It's a sandy strip of land that sticks thirty-five miles out into the Atlantic Ocean. It was formed by the glaciers that slid down here from the north more than 12,000 years ago. An ice sheet, or glacier, forms when snow accumulates year after year with very little melting. As it grows, it slides over the land and picks up any bedrock underneath it. As it drags the boulders, it chisels away the land and grinds the material up into fine sand and gravel. As 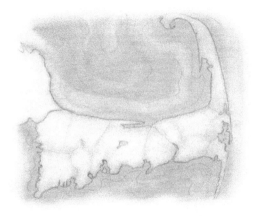 the earth warmed again, the glaciers melted and all the debris that advanced toward the south edge of the glacier was deposited here. That's how my favorite place, Cape Cod, and the islands of Martha's Vineyard and Nantucket were formed. At that time, Cape Cod was a very different place, with all sorts of strange creatures. In fact, they say at one time giant Mastodons, relatives of Wooly Mammoths, roamed near here. I'm glad they don't anymore. I'm not sure if they liked dogs. Those animals scare me. They're so big and hairy. I know all this because I hear Mom talk about it on her whale watch trips. She's also a whale biologist. Her being a whale biologist is great fun for me because often I get to go to work with her. I've been on a lot of whale watch trips and I have seen a lot of whales.

I remember my first trip. It was crazy. I had been on boats before.
I help Dad coach sailing at the local high school. So I'm on the
coach's boat all the time. I really like hanging out with those high
school kids. I'm the team mascot, but that's another story. Anyway,
I had never been on a boat like that before. It was more than 100
feet long and it had two decks, hundreds of tourists, and even
other dogs! I'm usually the only dog on the coach's boat, so I'm
not sure I liked having other dogs around one bit. That big boat
moved a lot differently than the coach's boat. I have to admit I was
uncomfortable, but once I noticed two other dogs had boarded the
boat, I showed them and got my sea legs fast. It was bumpy that day
and my stomach wasn't feeling too great, but the galley guy, Scuba
Steve, offered me a few hotdogs and that settled my stomach fast.
I just kept telling myself, "I can do this; I'm a Cape Cod dog." In
fact, I've often been referred to as a sea dog. I CAN'T get seasick.
Dad took me into the wheelhouse to visit with Captain Pete while
Mom entertained the passengers. I fell asleep on Dad's lap and while
I slept, I could hear the gulls and dreamt I was chasing them on the

14

beach. I dream of this a lot. In real life, I never catch them. They fly away before I can reach them but in my dreams I always get at least one, and then suddenly I wake up. In real life, I'm much more skilled at catching squirrels and rabbits. I'm not sure why everyone gets so upset when I bring them home. Just once I wish they would be proud. I know I am. I guess it's because they love *all* animals, but let's face it: Dogs rule.

Anyway, suddenly the boat stopped, I found myself in the middle of the ocean and everyone was so excited. Nancy the Naturalist (aka Mom) said, "Whales at two o'clock!" Everyone ran to the right side of the boat. She explained, "To point out where things are, we will pretend the boat is a clock. The bow—that's the front—is twelve o'clock. The back, the stern, is six o'clock. The left, port side, is nine o'clock and starboard side is three o'clock." Easy enough. When all the passengers moved to starboard, the boat leaned over to one side. It felt like it was going to tip, but I wasn't scared. With all of my boating experience, I knew boats have keels to help keep them stable in the water. I'll bet those other two dogs didn't know that. I eyed the beagle that was looking pretty nervous. I knew this because he peed right there all over the deck. How embarrassing! He definitely was not a sea dog like me. I looked to two o'clock and suddenly this big spray came off the water, and WHAT A STINK! I think, so this is it? This is a whale, the biggest animal on earth? Creature of the deep? Acrobat of the sea? Leviathan? How about STINK BOMB OF THE OCEAN!? Why don't you ever hear people call them that? I mean really, in all my dog years I had never smelled such a stink! Given the fact that they exchange 90 percent of the air they breathe and exhale at 300 miles per hour, have lungs the size of a compact car and eat over one ton of slimy fish a day, was it any wonder why their breath would be so RANCID! Crazy thing is nobody seemed to care. Everyone was so excited. They screamed and cheered. I guessed it's true about us dogs having a sense of smell 10,000 to 100,000 times more sensitive than the average human. I made eye contact with the other dog, a pug. Not only were his eyes bulging out more than usual, but they were tearing up because the smell was so bad.

Mom said, "It's a cow-calf pair, a mom with her baby." The baby was a perfect miniature of the mother. It was like seeing a black toy poodle walking alongside a standard poodle only instead of being six pounds and sixty pounds, they are ten tons and fifty tons! I had to admit that the whales were fun to watch. The calf kept rolling around and flipping its white flipper, while the mom went down to search for food. My mom told the crowd the baby didn't need to search for food because it was still nursing and is gaining almost 100 pounds a day by drinking its mother's milk! Her milk is 40 to 50 percent milk fat. The milk people buy in the store is no more than four percent. No wonder they grow so fast! While the calf waited for its mother to come back up, it seemed to be playing with us as it came along the side of the boat, rolled to its side and slapped its flipper on the water. Finally, the mother returned to the surface, and they swam side by side. Then they lifted their tails and disappeared into the deep. I'm not sure why they call those things tails because they're not shaped like any tail *I've* ever seen. We waited for them to come back up. Suddenly, at three o'clock, right next to our boat, they both jumped clear up out of the water together and came down in the biggest splash I had ever seen! Now I have done belly flops into the water before but nothing like this. It was what Mom called a double breach!

And that was it. My first whale watch adventure and I was hooked. Since then, I have been on countless whale watches. I know tons about whales, and I'm pretty accustomed to the boat. I have been out in all sorts of weather and my stomach is fine as long as I get a few hot dogs to settle it. I've even had a few chili dogs but Mom and Dad won't let me have those anymore after one particular gassy night. Sure, the chili dogs might give me a lot of gas, but it's no worse than stinky whale breath!

Shelby Visits the Dune Shacks of Provincetown

It looked like they were going somewhere again. They were packing their clothes, a cooler, the truck. I didn't like this because sometimes I get left behind. Fortunately, I saw Mom pack my food and toys, and I began to bark with excitement! It looked like I was going with them, but where? Dad had his guitar, and Mom had some books and beach chairs. It looked like we were headed to the beach but what was all the packing about? We hopped in the truck and headed north. We must be going to Provincetown, I thought. We go there a lot for walks, lunch, dinner, whale watching and (my favorite) ice cream. I love a small vanilla cone! I realized we were headed to the dune shacks of Provincetown. We had done a lot of day trips out there, hiking through the dunes, but this looked like we were going to have an overnight trip.

As our truck crested over the last hills of Truro, we saw one of my favorite views on all of Cape Cod. In front of us were the biggest sand dunes of the Cape, with the town of Provincetown in the background. To the left, we viewed a row of tiny cottages, with the beautiful blue Cape Cod Bay glistening in the sun beyond them. To the right we saw Pilgrim Lake, which at one time was the main harbor of this tiny town. After being cut off from the bay many years ago, the harbor became a shallow fresh water lake. Once we passed the lake, we pulled off the road. Mom jumped out with a key and opened the gate while Dad let some air out of the tires. They hopped in the truck and Dad put it into four wheel drive. He pulled the truck forward onto the sandy road. I never knew you could drive out here. It's hard enough running through the deep sand. Even with my paws spread wide, I always sunk in and the hills out here are huge. The sand blows around and forms these gigantic bowls that can be as deep as a hundred feet. I love to run up and down them. It's *so* hard and I get *so* tired, but it's so much fun! I love coming out here. The landscape is like nothing any dog has ever seen before, well except for maybe a Cape Cod coyote. Most of the sand out here comes from the eroding beaches of Eastham, where I live, and from Wellfleet. A lot of the sand gets carried out to sea, but some of it is carried north by ocean currents and wind and is deposited here. Not only does it create a beautiful landscape, but it also becomes a home for all sorts of wildlife. Some I like and some, well, not so much.

We bounced in the truck up and down the hills and through the sand until we reached a tiny shack called Annabelle. It's so small it's like a dog house for people. Inside was a bed, counter, small fridge and a gas burner for cooking. I was glad for that because I don't particularly care for cold hot dogs. I like them grilled. I thought this is what people must mean when they say they are roughing it! While Mom and Dad settled in, I explored. I loved all the smells, the sand, the salt air, the flowers. The rose hips are my favorite beach flower; they smell so sweet, just like candy. Deer, coyotes, foxes, raccoons and, of course, my favorite, rabbits were all out here. I could smell each one of them. As I made my way across the dunes, I heard the ocean and knew it was close. I leaped over the last dune and ran full speed down the steep hill where there was nothing but me and the surf, open sand, and lots of birds.

Before I left for my romp through the dunes, Mom and Dad specifically said, "No beach." I knew what that meant. I wasn't supposed to be down there and it's because of those birds. They call them "Piping Plovers." They are a threatened shore bird that was endangered because years ago they were hunted for their feathers. They are not hunted anymore, but over the years they have lost  a great deal of suitable habitat. They come to the outer beaches of Cape Cod to make nests and lay their eggs on the beach. They are protected here, so, hopefully, their populations will grow. The seashore rangers build little cages around their nests so the foxes, coyotes, and nice little dogs like me don't eat the eggs. I guess I understand it's important to protect them so they all don't die, but it makes some people around here angry because the rangers close the beaches. I've even seen bumper stickers around here that say "Piping Plovers taste like chicken!" That sure does make getting through one of those cages all the more tempting; after all, I love chicken. It's my favorite. I wondered if they really do taste like chicken. I trotted over to one of the wire cages and sniffed. Even though some sand got up my nose, I could smell them. They kind of *smelled* like chicken. Then I remembered, "No beach." I bet I could dig right under this cage. I saw the two little chicks in the nest. I thought, *What a great snack.* They peeped for their mom. They looked scared. I felt bad and remembered, "No beach." I started to dig as they peeped louder and louder. Suddenly I caught myself and thought, *What am I doing? I'm not a wild dog like a coyote. I am civilized. I know better.* I started to leave when this mom bird started dive-bombing around my head. I charged up the dune face, but the sand slipped from under my paws and I lost my grip. I fell flat on my muzzle and the mother Plover stuck her pointy beak into my ear and slapped me on the side of my head with her feathers. For a little bird, she was tough. I spread my paws, lunged forward and darted up the dune. When I made it to the top, she was gone, so I stopped to catch my breath. I didn't need to go to the beach just then anyway.

At home, I go to the beach everyday with my dad. He sits and plays his guitar while I explore and, boy, do I find all kinds of things, but that's another story. The Provincetown dunes were another adventure that I didn't get to have every day. There was plenty there to keep me busy, like chasing rabbits. I noticed a lot of them around. Just like me, they seemed to like the rose hips. I saw them eat the flowers and fruit. When I chased after them, they darted under the bushes to escape me, and that worked pretty well, I have to say. I'd even go after the rabbits in the bushes, but they had a lot of thorns that got stuck in my long furry tail. When I tried to pull them out, it hurt, or I couldn't reach them. I wasn't having much luck that day so I decided to move on. I stumbled across a dead something. Usually I eat the dead things I find, but I prefer to know what I'm eating. So instead of munching on it, I decided to store it for later. The problem with that was someone else might find it. Instead, I decided to claim it. First I leaned forward and rubbed the sides of my face on it. Then I rolled on top of it, rubbing my back and butt all over it. While on my back, I wiggled and inched my body like a worm from my ears to my tail. Once I knew my fine dog scent was all over it, I picked it up and carried it in my mouth trying to find the ideal spot for it. I found my way into the lowlands where there was a patch of cranberries, dug a hole, and buried it. With it well hidden, I could wait and think about what it must be, and, when I got really hungry, I could dig it up and eat it!

I made my way back to the dune shacks to check on Mom and Dad. They were content. Dad was writing some music, and Mom was in a sand chair, reading. I trotted over to check in to say hi before I continued my expedition. They were happy to see me as always and asked where I'd been. Did they really need to know about the beach? I didn't think so. I just panted and wagged my tail. They gave me a pat. Suddenly the look on Mom's face turned to disgust. She told Dad, "He stinks." Dad bent down to take a whiff and said, "Oh Shelby! My boy stinks!" They know me well. They decided I must have found something dead and rolled in it. Mom said, "He needs a bath or he's not sleeping with us tonight!" Now that was a problem, because the dune shacks have no electricity, no running water, no hose or shower. They were out of luck. I thought I smelled just fine and I hate baths. Unfortunately, what I didn't know was there was a pump that drew water right from the ground. I guessed the well was way under the sand in the earth. Dad went for my leash and I thought here goes my freedom. He put my leash on and walked me down to this metal thing sticking out of the sand. Mom got some dish detergent from the shack and a five gallon bucket and met us at the pump. Dad started pumping and the water poured out into the bucket. I was a bit thirsty, so I lapped some up. Ouch! I had never tasted water this cold before. It was so cold it hurt my teeth and made me sneeze. There was no way they were washing me with that ice water. I pulled and tried to break free, but they had me. They poured the water and lathered me up. I thought, *I really did it this time.* I dropped my head and tail and let them do what had to be done. Besides I didn't want to sleep alone tonight. As I sat cooperatively, Mom and Dad kissed and praise me and told me how good I was. I sure was sorry I had gotten myself into this mess, but I loved them too. After, Dad toweled me off and I sat in the sun and licked myself dry.

Later, we all sat enjoying the quiet together. The dunes are a peaceful place. No noise but the sounds of nature. The rest of the day was relaxing. We had a late dinner just before the sun went down, and, just after the sun set, we went to bed. It was fun; the three of us snuggled together in the tiny shack in the dunes by the sea. I sure was glad I had that bath.

The morning came quickly, and we were up with the sun. They drank their coffee and we all ate some breakfast. Dad announced "It's time for a beach walk!" I jumped to my feet and grabbed my ball. Mom grabbed her binoculars, and, believe it or not, she grabbed

24

my leash. Come on, you have got to be kidding me. What kind of beach walk was this going to be if I had to be on a leash? It's those darn tasty chickens, I mean Piping Plovers! I gave her the "but I'll be a good dog" look. She didn't buy it. She thought my instinct to eat those tiny chicks would be too strong. If she only knew about the self-control I had yesterday, she'd be so impressed. I really was a good dog.

The walk was uneventful. Mom and Dad had fun. They spied some whale spouts through the binoculars ,and we watched seals playing in the surf. The seals I liked. They remind me of myself, a salty sea dog, who enjoyed the beach and rolling surf. I sniffed out a few good things like surf clams, sea sponges, even an old flip flop, but nothing too exciting like an old fish head. That was okay because I knew a place at home where I can find lots of those. But that's another story. I'll tell you about that later.

We hiked back up into the dunes. Mom took the breakfast dishes down to the pump for washing and Dad began to read. I poked around the shack. The deck around it was decorated with what Mom called gifts from the sea—like sea glass, driftwood, shells, old colorful buoys, and even whale bones. I knew they were bones from whales because I knew their smell. I decided I needed a change of scenery so I started to wander. I made my way through the beach grass, passed the beach plums, and headed down toward the scrub pine. I was in the lowlands again and found the cranberry patch I was in yesterday. I smelled that smell again and it finally hit me. It's a raccoon! It's a dead stinky raccoon! I dug it up and munched on what might have been an ear. It tasted kind of funky, but there was something about it I still liked. Proud of my find, I brought it back to the shack. Mom grabbed my collar and said, "Drop it Shelby!" Was she serious? No way was she taking this away, but I played along and dropped it at her feet. She released my collar and said, "Good boy, Shelby." But before she could lean over to pick it up, I grabbed it and ran like a fox terrier through the open fields. She tried to chase me, but there was no way she was going to catch me. Dad told her to forget about it and they started to laugh. Once I was at a safe distance, I decided to choke it all down before they tried to take it away again. They cringed as they watched me swallow the last of it, the tail. Best for last! They warned me and said, "You are going to get sick, Shelby." There was something that tasted a little odd about it, but I ate it just the same. I was afraid I'd lose it.

Like the day before, the rest of the afternoon was uneventful, quiet. Mom cooked, and they offered me the leftover hamburgers, but I wasn't really interested. We went to bed and that's when the problems began. My stomach was grumbling so loud that both my dad and I couldn't sleep. He's a light sleeper. It grumbled more and more, and it started to hurt. I needed out of this dog house and fast! Dad knew I was in trouble. He said it was worse than the time I ate the chili dogs. He grabbed my leash and out we went, just in time. I eventually felt a lot better so we went back in. We fell asleep, but, about a half-hour later, my mouth started filling with saliva and I felt like I was going to puke. I needed to get out again and fast. I scratched at the door but before I could let out a bark, I lost it. That nasty raccoon, or what was left of it, came up. Dad finally let me out, and I couldn't stop puking. Mom cleaned up the mess, but the dog house reeked. They decided I needed to spend the night outside because just when we thought I was better my stomach started up again. They wouldn't let me stay outside alone because they were afraid the coyotes would come get me, so they stayed outside with me in shifts. I figured if the coyotes did come after me, all I would need to do was puke up a little more of that rancid raccoon. That should make them scatter real fast.

My stomach finally settled and we all got some rest. Sleeping outside was neat. The full-moon cast grey shadows all along the sand. You could hear a fog horn in the distance and see the flash of the Cape

Cod Lighthouse's beacon bounce off the dunes. Dad was asleep beside me in a chair. I felt at peace and even with a slight rumble in my stomach, I thought, *I love being a Cape Cod dog.*

Shelby Kayaks First Encounter Beach

The day was a typical Cape Cod summer morning. Mom was up early preparing breakfast and chatting with our B&B guests. They were a nice family from Italy. Dad and I were off to the donut shop, where we go every morning. Dad gets his coffee and gets caught up on the local news, where the fish are biting, where the biggest lobsters have been caught—that sort of thing. Just the other day, some diver caught a thirty-one-pounder! I had no idea they could grow that big! It takes a lobster about five to seven years to grow big enough to be legally harvested. At that point they are about 1 ¼ pounds. After that they grow more slowly as they get larger. At that rate that thirty-one-pound lobster could have been close to a hundred years old! The divers brought it up to take a picture  of it to prove they caught it, and then put it back. They didn't feel right about killing something that managed to live that long. I have to agree with that way of thinking.

Some days, Dad's in the coffee shop a long time. I try to be patient but it's hard when I know he's coming out with a few of those doughnut holes for me. To pass the time, I sit in the truck and watch the people go in and out. They seem happy and visit with one another. I love to watch the kids sit outside and eat their doughnuts. Their eyes light up as they take their first big bite. Boston Cream seems to be a favorite and so does chocolate with rainbow sprinkles. Before they finish, half the doughnut always ends up on them or on the ground. If I could just get out of this truck and clean up the spills like I do at home. That's how I help Mom out, by cleaning up the spills. I love when young families stay at our B&B. Even without their spills, I am usually bound to get some special snacks. People often will visit Chatham or Provincetown and stop in the gourmet pet shop and bring me home special snacks. Lucky for me, there's also a shop near my house, so guests are always buying me something delicious. My favorites are the Buddy Biscuits or even better, the Woofie Pies! Like Mom always says, "Special treats for a special dog!"

Anyway, once the guests are cared for and off for the day, we are off for our own fun. The rule of the summer is we get to play tourist once a week and today's the day. We are off to First Encounter Beach. I go there almost every day, but today it's a picnic and kayak ride along the beach and up into the estuary. It's called First Encounter Beach because it's where the Pilgrims encountered the Native Americans, so it's a famous place. Not many people realize the Pilgrims landed on Cape Cod first before settling in Plymouth. They spent a month in Provincetown, and explored the shores of Truro, Wellfleet and Eastham. Unfortunately, they had hard time accessing fresh water here. On one clear day, they looked west, and in the distance saw a large piece of land and decided to take the Mayflower across Cape Cod Bay to Plymouth. But before they headed to Plymouth, they had many interesting experiences with the Native Americans.

One such experience took place on a cold December day. Some members of the Mayflower crew formed a team in search of fresh water. They made their way deep into Cape Cod Bay, off the shore of what is now called Eastham, my home, and spent the night on the beach. They set up a barricade because they knew the Native Americans were nearby. They fell asleep but were awaken by arrows sailing into their camp. It was still dark. Some men grabbed their guns and shot into the air and the natives ran off. Even though the Pilgrims had encountered the Native Americans before, this was the most memorable meeting, so this area was named First Encounter Beach.

I've had my own memorable experience around here, including a meeting with a skunk. I have seen and chased a lot of skunks before, but the one I met this particular night was truly unforgettable. Unlike the night of the Pilgrims' encounter, this night was hot, humid, and sticky. It was back before we had the B&B, when our house was just a small cottage. We slept with the windows open. Even the front door was open, but the screen door was closed, or so I thought. Anyway, I woke up because I could smell a musky ferret; at least I thought that's what I smelled. I knew what ferrets smell like, because I lived with one for several years. Philippe lived with Mom and Dad before I moved in. When I came along, I didn't waste any time and laid down the rules and showed him who was boss. Philippe would bounce sideways throughout the house. He even showered once a week with my Dad. That was kind of weird but it did decrease his stink! We chased each other around the house a lot. One thing that always impressed me about that weasel was that he knew how to feed himself. He would climb into the kitchen cabinet, find the Cheerios box, pull them onto the floor and eat the cereal. I would walk into the kitchen and see his little ferret butt sticking out of the Cheerios box. I'd help myself to some Cheerios too.

He was annoying and got under my feet a lot. He acted like he owned the place. One day I got tired of his attitude and chased him into the living room. He climbed up the couch and leaped onto the coffee table. With him up there, we were eye to eye, nose to nose.

31

I nipped at his face, and the little weasel grabbed my nose with his sharp teeth and hung on. I couldn't get him off until I put my muzzle to the floor and pushed him off with my big paw. He drew blood and I still have a scar. Once I got him off, I squished him with my paw like a pancake. Don't worry, I didn't hurt him. Ferrets are very flexible, but I did hold him down for a long time. After that, he figured out who was top dog!

Anyway, I'll get back to my skunk story. I thought the screen door was closed, and noticed a musky smell, and heard some scratching near the front door. Since I knew my family was sleeping, I needed

to respond. I looked out the door and saw what looked like a big black-and-white ferret with a Mohawk haircut! I thought, there is no way I am sharing this house with another stink bomb! I figured I would jump up on the door to scare it away. So I let out a big growl and lunged against the door. But the door wasn't closed all the way, and, when I lunged, it swung open. I fell out the door and down the steps, and that nasty skunk lifted its tail and sprayed right into the house. Needless to say, everyone woke up and the house stunk for a few days. The funny thing of it was, because I fell, the spray went right over my head and completely missed me! Being the agile dog I am, I recovered quickly. After all the commotion was over, we all tried to get some rest, but it was tough with that awful skunk smell in the house. Since that first encounter, I've learned to keep my distance from skunks.

And now today we're headed to First Encounter Beach. We put the kayak into the water and were ready to jump in. But before we jumped in, Mom pulled out that embarrassing life jacket. I can't believe she makes me wear that thing. How many dogs, let alone Golden Retrievers, have you seen in a life jacket? Not only is it embarrassing, but it's real uncomfortable. I feel like an overweight stuffed marshmallow—all puffed out and awkward. She says it's for my safety because, even though I consider myself a sea dog, to be honest with you, I don't really like being *in* the water and Mom knows this. I love to be *on* it but *in* it, not so much. I guess it's the Chow Chow in me. Chows are not water dogs but Goldens are, so sometimes I feel a little confused.

We cruised along the beach and paddled up into the estuary. We drank lots of water and ate many snacks. We even had some Cape Cod potato chips. I love chips. They're my favorite. As we paddled, we watched an osprey fly overhead. Ospreys are fish hawks, big birds of prey that feed on fish. Their nests, at three to four feet deep, are huge. Ospreys build them on big poles that people have erected

for them. Years ago, osprey numbers dropped because pesticides weakened the shells of their eggs and new chicks were not hatched. Like the Piping Plovers, they became endangered, but the osprey story is a success story. Since they became protected and we stopped using the pesticides and helped give them nice areas to nest in, they have successfully reproduced and the population is increasing. I hope the same will happen to the Piping Plovers.

Ospreys are majestic birds. They are regal, busy birds that constantly work together. The male bird searches for building material for the nest. He presents it to his mate, who furiously works to arrange it just so. They've got to get it right because in just a few short weeks she will lay her eggs and they will raise their family here. They take turns hunting and watching over the nest. On this particular day, we had quite a show; one was on the nest while the other was hunting. We watched the hunter circle and swoop down. Just as it reached the water, it released its talons but it came up empty. This happened a few more times. It was fun to watch, but I kind of felt bad. This bird was working hard and it had a family to feed! As we paddled closer to the nest, the other bird standing guard seemed to get nervous, so we backed off and just floated in our kayak and watched. Suddenly, the hunter bird swooped down right in front of our little boat, hit the water with its feet, and came up with a herring in its grasp. As it pulled up and circled around, the fish floundered. We watched the osprey fly off and disappear. We thought the bird would bring its catch back to the nest but it didn't. Wild dogs bring their kill right back to their family, although sometimes we feed ourselves first. Maybe that's what the osprey was doing. Sure enough, about five minutes later, we saw the bird carrying a half eaten fish with its guts hanging out. It landed in the nest. The other bird had a nibble and flew off while the hunter tore into the fish. It was hard to see into the nest, but it looked like the adult bird was feeding the chicks. We were so excited. Mom and Dad said we were lucky to witness something like this. They said it's one of the benefits of living on Cape Cod.

The rest of the day was uneventful and relaxing. We paddled up toward the bike trail until we couldn't get much farther. As the tide turned, Mom and Dad stopped paddling and let the tide pull us back out toward the beach. When the sounds of the paddling stopped, they quit talking and enjoyed the silence. Riding the current felt good, and all we heard were the sounds of nature.

After a few hours in the sun and on the water, we decided to top off this great day with a quick trip to the ice cream shop. Now that's a benefit of living on Cape Cod. I love a small vanilla cone! I think to myself, *Special treats, for a special dog, on a special day.*

Shelby Romps Along the Outer Beaches of Cape Cod

A Cape Cod dog spends a lot of time on the beach. The beach is a special place. Not just for dogs but for people too. Around here in the summer, people flock there. I used to go to the beach on warm summer days in the afternoon, but now I just go either early morning, right after our trip to the coffee shop, or later in the afternoon, after the hordes of people have left. It's much quieter and there are fewer things for me to get in trouble with.

During the day, it's a different place: families, beach chairs, umbrellas, music, and, of course, snacks. On a beach like that, I can always find some Fritos or chips in the sand. Strangers love me, and if I sit long enough, lift my ears, tilt my head, and wag my tail, I am bound to get a ham-and-cheese sandwich from some unsuspecting kid. I take it quickly and run since the parents usually jump from their chairs to chase me away. It's kind of a game I play. I'm not sure what's more fun, getting the treats or seeing the parents freak out. I could do it all day, even if I'm not hungry. But, me not hungry? How often does *that* happen?

The beach is a great place for a dog because there is so much to do. One thing I would never do, which I see a lot of other dogs do, is lift my leg on a blanket. That's just not right. I have to admit I've been tempted, especially when I smell another dog's scent, but I don't. Like I said, it's just not right. A quiet beach in the early morning or afternoon is more of a challenge for a dog, but I am up for it.

So many foul smells, so many things to eat. One of my favorite is a dead fish. Once I even found a dead dolphin. I ripped its fin off and charged down the beach as Mom and Dad chased me to try to get it away from me. I'm not sure if they were upset because it was a dolphin or they were afraid I might eat it. So what if I ate it? I'm a dog; that's part of what we do.

Just hanging out on the beach can be fun, too. You never know what might come your way. One night Mom and Dad and a few friends took the SUV out to the Race Point Lighthouse for a barbeque to watch the sun go down. It was nice and quiet, with not many people around. Race Point is part of the National Seashore, and the sign says, "Dogs must be leashed!" How fun is that? Being tethered to a beach chair is no fun. I whined a lot, hoping to be released. Unfortunately, Mom and Dad are all about following the rules, but sometimes I get lucky, like this night.

Being tied to that beach chair was a real drag until Dad decided to stand up. Just at that same moment what do I notice but this little harbor seal inching itself onto the beach. Now I have seen seals before but never out of the water. In the water they cruise along the shore. They look like black labs but you never see them fetching balls. They seem far too sophisticated for that. This one looked like a big giant worm undulating along the sand. To tell you the truth, up until this point, seals never bothered me; in fact, I enjoy watching them. But for some reason on this particular day, I got crazy mad. I remember thinking, is this sea dog coming up here to steal one of my hotdogs? No way! So I did it! Just as Dad stood up, I lunged forward and ran toward the water with that stupid beach chair in tow. It bounced along the sand as I raced to the shore. As it bounced, it pulled me back, but I dug my claws in the sand and pushed forward. I think I even took out a few sandcastles along the way! Well, you should have seen that seal move. For an animal with no legs, it scooted along pretty darn fast, and, lucky for him, it did! Although, thinking back now, I'm not sure what I planned to do if I ever did reach it before it hit the water. Like I said, I really do like seals.

We have a lot of seals around Cape Cod, mostly Grey Seals and Harbor Seals. In the winter, we even get ice seals around here, like Ringed Seals, Hooded Seals, and Harp Seals. These are seals that usually live in the colder waters of the north but some make their way down here. They say that, as the seal population grows, the weaker ones get pushed down here to the south. Like me, seals can be very territorial, but, once they establish some order, it's not unusual to see different species hanging out together. There are a lot of seals along the National Seashore. Whatever beach we go to, we usually see their round heads bobbing in the water. Their heads look so round because they don't have any ear flaps. That's one thing that makes them different from sea lions: no external ears. They also can't rotate their hind flippers like sea lions. That's why they look like big fat worms out of the water. They can't walk. What I found most impressive is their thick pointy whiskers. I would love to have whiskers like that. They use their whiskers like fingers to search for fish, clams, and other molluscs buried in the sand. I guess I don't really need whiskers like that, but I would like to have them. I think they're cool.

Needless to say, I stopped chasing that little Harbor Seal at the water's edge once it hit the surf. Seals can have the ocean; they are better adapted to it. I'll keep my paws in the sand.

Shelby Sails Cape Cod Bay

Today was one of those days when we got to play tourist again. We were going to sail the Hindu. This is one of Mom and Dad's favorite things to do. The Hindu is an 80-foot wooden schooner that was built in 1925. She has quite a history. In the 1930s, she carried spices between India and Boston. During World War II, she was part of the coastal patrol in the U.S. Navy. After the war, the mounted machine gun on her foredeck was removed and she was sold to Captain Al Avellar, who used her as one of the world's first whale watching boats. Today, the Hindu is operated by Captain Kevin Foley, A.K.A. Captain Foggy. He has been sailing on the Hindu since he was twelve years old. He's a lot older now and is what people on the docks refer to as an old "Salty Dog." I try not to take offense at this because he is not of the canine kind! Foggy restored the old schooner to take people and cute little sea dogs like me on sailing excursions in and around Provincetown Harbor. From where we park in town, you can see the Hindu's great wooden masts.

We began our walk down the wharf. This is always a good time on its own—great people and animal watching. Once, I saw a man walking two cats, one on a leash and the other in a baby carriage. Imagine a cat pretending to be a dog and another, a child! I told you it's quite a show on this pier. There's even a beagle who wears a beret and lives on a small sailboat. His name is Mate and he helps run Dog Gone Sailing Charters. He seems to like wearing the hat. He struts down the pier like he owns the place, and everyone falls all over him. Someone should be honest and tell him how ridiculous he looks in that beret. A dog in a hat! That's almost as bad as a dog in a life jacket! Which reminds me of another reason why I like sailing the Hindu so much. Mom doesn't make me wear that foolish life jacket. That's not to say she didn't try. Thankfully, Dad talked her out of it. He explained the boat is a lot bigger than a kayak and it would be much more difficult for me to fall overboard.

That's one thing I really love about Dad; he has this way of looking out for my dogness. We understand each other. That's why I love riding in the truck together. It doesn't matter where we are heading, the beach, the dump, wherever; it's our alone time together. Me, Dad, and the truck. It's quality time. Although, I must say I do like going to that drive-up window at the bank. The nice lady always passes us an envelope with a small Milk Bone in it!

Captain Foggy is also a good source of dog treats. Whenever he welcomes me aboard, he heads to the galley and returns with a Milk Bone. What a great way to start a sailing excursion, and I am certain more treats will follow. There are lots of people on this boat and most came with coolers. A dog like me can only imagine what might be tucked away inside. It won't be long before we get under way and I can turn on my charm to earn some snacks. Before we set sail, Captain Foggy filled us in on all the important safety instructions. He took the wheel and commanded, "Cast off the lines!" We motored away from the pier, passed the breakwater, and we headed into the wind. Mom and a few others grasped the halyard and pulled when Captain Foggy shouted, "Hoist the mainsail." Once the sail reached the top of the mast, they stopped and tied off the lines. They were out of breath. It looked like hard work.

Once the sails were set, we all settled in and relaxed. The only sounds we heard were the quiet conversations among friends, the rippling water as the hull cut through the sea, and steady wind along the sails. It was peaceful, so I sat and just took it all in for awhile. I like the feel of the wind moving through the fur along my ears. I listened to the conversations of my parents; often, they were answering questions about me. Passengers commented on my red coat and asked, "What kind of dog is he? His color is beautiful. He's a perfect size, not too big, and he seems to have a nice disposition." I pretended not to listen. They eventually got off topic, moving on to something other than me. That's when I decided to scope out the passengers and make the rounds. By now, people were comfortable and started to open those coolers.

I noticed a nice, young family—a couple with two children. One looked about eighteen months, the other about three years old. A family like that was bound to have some of those cheesy goldfish snacks I love so much! That's an easy target for sure. The baby was in a backpack, and the three-year-old was in a harness with a leash attached. Boy, I felt for that kid. I guessed that was one way of keeping track of him. Personally, I thought *that* kid should be in a life jacket. I mean, he could barely walk as it is, let alone on a moving sailboat! If he went over, I really didn't want to have to jump in after him, but I would if I needed to. If I see anyone in distress, it's just my nature to do what I can to protect. I wouldn't give it a second thought to jump in to rescue him. I just hoped I had some Newfoundland genes that kick in. They were bred to be water rescue dogs.

There was also an older couple who seems to know Captain Foggy. They must have been "townies," which means they are probably Portuguese. Most people who live year-round in Provincetown have family who were originally from Portugal. They came to Cape Cod to fish. They have a lot of traditional foods, but my favorite is linguica. It's a spicy sausage they eat on many occasions; and going on a day sail in the bay is as good as an occasion as any. Just as I was thinking this, out comes this bowl of linguica that had been marinated in a sweet and sour sauce, an interesting combination, and grilled. They offered some to Captain Foggy. I couldn't think of a better time to make my move. It was a pretty calm day, so I found it easy to trot along the deck to the stern. Soon as they saw me, they tossed me a few slices. That was real easy. I continued to sit and wait for more, but it didn't come. I whined a little but quickly got the look from Mom and knew it was time to move on.

Some people who have sandwiches share their chips with me. As I made my way toward the bow, I saw a nice lady pull out a cutting board from her tote bag. Then I smelled it; even out here in the midst of all this salt air, I smelled my favorite, a block of cheese. She was super-nice and sliced me off a few chunks, and I gobbled it up. I made my way to the bow and planted myself like a figurehead. It didn't get much better than this: eating cheese on an old wooden schooner running down wind. The wind was at my back, out of the southwest at fifteen knots on a perfect Cape Cod summer day. It felt good to be me.

From this perspective, I had a perfect view of what was ahead. I saw a lot of small splashes. With all my whale watch experience, I knew exactly what I was seeing. It was a pod of Atlantic White Sided Dolphins. I barked and looked back at Mom and Dad. They alerted everyone else to what I saw. Capt. Foggy caught us a nice puff of wind that sailed us forward into the pod. There had to be hundreds of them! This was so much fun! When we got into the middle of the pod, I looked past my paws down into the water under the bow and saw a bunch of them riding our bow waves. They weaved their sleek bodies in and out and every few seconds one surfaces for a quick breath of air. I looked all around us and turned toward the stern just when one of them jumped clear up out of the water. Mom says sometimes they leap like that to look for birds. Birds sometimes mean fish just below the surface, so it's a way to find food. I think they just do it for fun and just because they can. Just like dogs. There are lots of things dogs do, just because we can. For example, we eat

dirt. I don't really like dirt but it's something to do if I'm bored. Seeing dolphins in the harbor like this is not an everyday occurrence, so we were very lucky. Locals around here sometimes get concerned when they see dolphins so close to shore, but not in Provincetown Harbor. It's the second deepest natural harbor in the world. But when the pods head for the shallows of Wellfleet and Eastham, it's time for concern.

Cape Cod is a hot spot for the mass stranding of cetaceans. What that means is large groups of dolphins or whales will swim to shore and beach themselves together, all at the same time. It's really sad because most of them die if they're not suspended in the water. The weight of their body on the sand makes it too difficult for them to breathe. They struggle and die. Fortunately, these dolphins looked super healthy and sure do have a lot of energy. We took pictures and someone noticed many of the dolphins had tags on their dorsal fins. I thought that was pretty weird but it made Mom so excited. She took more pictures of the tagged dolphins and explained to our crew why this is so important. Oftentimes when the dolphins strand, a local rescue organization tries to save as many as they can. The members push the dolphins back out to sea, but, before they do, they tag them. If the tagged animals are spotted again offshore, they know they were the animals that were once beached and know how successful their efforts were. Mom told everyone how important this information was and who the scientists were that they needed to send their pictures off to. We were all certain that the scientists would be thrilled!

The pod was big and there were animals of all different sizes and ages. There were even some newborns. You can tell because you can still see what my Mom calls "fetal folds." They are wrinkles in their skin from when they are folded up in the mother dolphin's belly. The dolphins appear to have gills! But they don't because they're mammals, not fish. These dolphins were so little that they looked like little footballs. They were perfect little miniatures of their mothers. It was fun to see them together. They sure were cute!

After a while, the dolphins moved on to play with some faster boats. After all, the boat we were in was just a sailboat and couldn't create as many fun waves for the dolphins to play in. After a few glorious hours of sailing, we headed back in. That day was a perfect example of what I love about Cape Cod. All we wanted today was simple pleasure, but whatever we do always seem to turn out to be an adventure. Not only is sailing on the Hindu always a blast, but it feels good to know our experiences will help humans better understand animals. I wonder if anyone will remember it was a little red Cape Cod dog standing on the bow of an old wooden ship that spotted those dolphins first.

Shelby's Big Confession

I have a confession to make. I think I have been somewhat misleading. Up until now, I have made it sound like our family is just me, Mom, and Dad, but to be perfectly honest with you, there is more to the story. There's the cat. Yup, that's right, I said *the cat*. I haven't mentioned her because most of the time I'd like to pretend she doesn't exist. She came into the picture long after I got there. I have no idea why Mom and Dad adopted her. Mom had been telling Dad for years she wanted a cat. He said no, but one day she came home with one anyway. I didn't understand. Wasn't I enough? Dad said Mom wanted a cat because she grew up with cats. Anyway, the cat's name is Taj and my relationship with her...well let's just say that it's complicated.

After our first meeting, I never thought she'd stick around. I chased her all around that house. It was crazy. I had her hanging from the ceiling upside down. I didn't know cats could do that! I kept getting in trouble, but it wasn't my fault! If she didn't run, I wouldn't chase her, but, let's face it, she's not too bright. I'd give her a threatening look, she'd scamper away, and off I'd go after her. I have to admit she's pretty quick but there have been a few times where I have actually caught that feisty feline. That's when I really got in trouble and not just with my parents but with her, Taj. That feline's got some claws! Whenever she got away, she'd run into some small spot that I couldn't fit into, like under a bed. I wish she'd stay there but, unfortunately, she didn't.

So here we are today, eight years later and Mom and Dad say Taj and I have a love/hate relationship. I call it a hate/hate relationship. Although, she does seem somewhat intrigued by me. I can't say I blame her. I know I'm an interesting dog, but must she sniff my face? Sometimes when I'm relaxed and resting at the foot of the bed, she walks over and sniffs my whole body especially my face, ears and muzzles, and I let her. She seems to know when I'll tolerate it. One of these days, just to freak her out, I should snap at her. But I'm not nasty like that, unlike her. One minute she's making that purring sound and rubbing her body against my legs like she loves me and the next thing you know she's swatting me in the face with those nasty claws! And I'm just minding my own business! Every so often, Dad tells Mom, "Your cat is whacked," and I have to say, I agree.

Taj follows my Mom all around the house and often gets locked in the basement or in one of the guest bedrooms. It's pretty funny because she can't get out. I hear her cry, even when Mom and Dad don't. Sometimes it can be hours before they notice she's "missing." She's strictly a house cat, but there have been a few times she's even been locked out of the house by accident, mostly at night.

Now that I'm older, sometimes I can't make it through the night without going to the bathroom. I wake Dad and he puts me on my run to pee. I bark when I'm done and he lets me back in. Taj will follow us out without Dad knowing and more than once she has gotten herself locked out! Did I already mention she is not too swift? So she sits at the slider meowing to be let back in. By this time, Dad is back asleep and Mom, well nothing wakes her up, even that awful feline screeching. So what do you think I do? Actually, you might be surprised. First, I sit and pretend I'm sleeping. The screeching continues, so I walk over to the door and stare at her. This makes her even crazier. Her cries turn to moans and at this point she's pretty ticked off at me. Then I get to thinking about all the coyotes in the neighborhood. Being a fellow canine, I know they would see her as an excellent midnight snack. I've even thought of it myself a few times. That would surely shut her up. I look at her and the desperation in her eyes is quite compelling, so I put my muzzle against the screen door and slide it open; quickly she scampers in. At last she feels safe, the moaning stops and I'm thinking finally I can get some sleep. In the morning, Mom finds the slider open and tells Dad that he must have left the slider open last night and how lucky they are the cat didn't get out. If she only knew how good a dog I really am. How many other dogs would have rescued a cat that they didn't even like from the neighborhood coyotes? I really am a good boy! Sometimes I wish that cat could talk. On second thought, it's probably just as well she can't. Like I said, it's all very complicated.

Shelby's Sea-cret Garden

Whenever there are cats around, I always seem to get into trouble. Most cats in the neighborhood know enough to keep their distance from my property. I established the boundaries quite some time ago but, just recently, there's a new cat in town. She showed up this spring. I found her poking around my backyard so I chased her up a tree. One day when I was home all alone, she had the nerve to come right up on my back deck. I lunged against the sliding glass door. That scared her! I already tolerate one cat around here; there's no way I'm putting up with two! Since then, she hasn't stepped one rotten feline paw into my yard.

One day while I was taking my daily romp up the dirt road, I discovered where she lived. Turns out she lives with this nice lady who leaves her doors wide open. She's been very friendly to me and even lets me in the house to eat. She offers me dog biscuits, but, to be honest, I prefer the cat food. I thought she liked me and we had a good thing going until, one day, she left this note at my house.

"Dear Mr. and Mrs. Peck,

Would you please try to keep your dog home for a while? He is being a terrible nuisance lately. He is at my house constantly and has learned how to push the screen slider open. He comes in and eats all the cat's dry food and then proceeds to the kitchen and eats all her canned food. If it is a newly opened can he just picks it up and walks away with it. This has been happening a couple of times a day and it is getting

53

expensive with the cost of cat food. He is not afraid of me and even if I catch him, I cannot get him to leave. And, of course, the cat is screaming at him, which also does not faze him in the least. I have no idea how to keep him out of here and this has been going on since the warm weather came. Please try to help me out here.
Thank you, Mrs. Eldredge"

Well after that, needless to say, I was grounded. My dad tried to smooth things over and bought her some cat food to replace what I had eaten. I wish he'd buy me some of that cat food; it tasted fishy and I love seafood. After all, I'm a Cape Cod dog.

I grew up on seafood. Lobsters are my favorite. I get a lot of them. Dad is a scuba diver, so he catches lobsters every week. We eat lobster everything: lobster stew, lobster bisque, lobster rolls, lobster salad. I like it all ways, but my favorite is just plain old steamed lobster. And to think, the Native Americans used lobsters as fertilizer! It was considered a poor man's food. Now it's what people eat only on special occasions because it's so expensive. But we enjoy it often.

Dad dives in a special spot he calls his "garden" and brings up a bunch. Sometimes he takes me with him for the ride. Sometimes Mom goes, too. She and I kayak in Dad's "garden" while Dad scuba dives. Just last week we did that. Mom was paddling and came upon an enormous Grey Seal eating a big striped bass. The seal let us come real close to watch him eat. We know it was a "he" because he had a great big head. Females' heads are smaller.

They call Grey Seals horse-head seals because males have a head that looks like a horse. We watched him for about ten minutes eating the fish. That's how long it took him to eat it. When we first saw him, the fish was still alive. We saw the tail flapping around. The seal bit into it and shook it hard; soon after, the fish stopped flapping. Then the seal held on to it sideways between his flippers like it was

54

an ear of corn and started munching on its head. You could hear the bones crackle. Then he tore open the belly. We were floating so close. I could actually smell the fish. I could feel myself getting

hungry and I started to drool. Then he did something really cool. In one swift move, he slid his sharp teeth all along one side of the fish and pulled the meat off the fish in one final swoop. He filleted it. Up until now I have only seen the fishermen do this on the charter boats with a knife. This seal did it with only his teeth! Maybe this is how the fishermen learned how to do it. People learn amazing things from us animals. After that I expected him to flip the fish over to the other side and do the same thing. I thought he might leave the head and bones behind; after all, that's what people do. But the seal and I know the head and bones are the best part! He tore into the other side and ate it bit by bit. When the meat was gone, he started munching the head again. He tried choking it down head first. You could see the tail sticking out of his mouth. I think it was still too big because it seemed to get stuck about half-way down, so he choked it back up and took a few more bites off the head again.

Then, in three big gulps, it went down with the tail sticking out of his mouth. He made one last gulp, and it was gone. Best for last, that's what I always say!

Thinking about my dad's garden got me hungry and thinking about my own "garden." Mine is stocked with plenty of seafood, too. A few months back, I was on my usual neighborhood romp when I smelled something real fishy coming from a neighbor's yard. It was the yard of a different neighbor, not the cat neighbor. I followed my nose and the scent got stronger as I made my way into their woods. I stumbled upon an area in the ground that smelled really good and it looked as if the ground had recently been dug up; so I started to dig. It didn't take long before I hit the jackpot. Under the dirt were a whole bunch of old dead fish heads! My favorite! I thought I must have died and gone to heaven. It must be true what they say, "All good dogs do go to heaven." I know I am a good dog! I was so overwhelmed there were so many of them. I wasn't sure what to do. I knew I couldn't eat all of them. I had to think quickly. What if someone else found my catch, someone like that nasty cat up the road? I decided the first thing I should do is eat one. I needed energy to carry out my plan, so I gobbled it down. Now it was time for some quick work. I picked one up and carried it into the woods of my own backyard, dug a hole and buried it for safe keeping.

So that was my plan. I shuttled them over, one by one, from the neighbor's yard to mine. I was on my last one when Dad looked out the window and saw me walking down the street with a giant sea bass sticking out of my mouth. He called me over so I surrendered it to his feet. I handed it over pretty easily, because I knew there were a lot more where that came from. He and Mom were shocked and couldn't figure out where I had gotten it. It made for great dinner conversation that night and several weeks after. Although, they never caught on to where the fish were coming from, they knew I continued to eat them day after day. My fish breath was a give-away. I ate them all in a week or two. When I finally ran out, I was disappointed. So I headed next door again and found a fresh batch. It seems my neighbor is an old sea dog himself, and now, like Dad, I have a "garden" of my own.

Shelby Goes Over the Bridge

Today is an unusual day. We have no B & B guests for a few days. So Mom and Dad decide to get off Cape to get a change of scenery and we head to Boston. That's another thing that makes Cape Cod so great: its close proximity to a beautiful historic seaside city. To get there, we need to cross over the Cape Cod Canal. The canal cuts through a narrow neck of land that joined Cape Cod to mainland Massachusetts, making Cape Cod an island. Its purpose was to shorten the trade route between New York City and Boston by 62 miles. The canal was constructed in 1909 and completed in 1916. It was later widened and is now the widest sea level canal in the world.

To cross the canal, we travel over the Sagamore Bridge to get to Boston and visit my grandparents. They are Mom's parents and are nice. I love when they visit us on Cape Cod. They like to take long walks, especially my Grandpa, and he always takes me! I think they prefer visiting me rather than me visiting them. I guess you can say I've developed a bit of a history at their house and let's just say it hasn't always been good.

I remember the first time I visited. It was in the summer, shortly after I was adopted. Mom and Dad thought they'd get a change of scenery that day, too. They wanted to see a rocky coastline instead of sandy Cape Cod. So they picked up Grandma and Grandpa at their house, but they decided to leave me behind.

Grandma didn't trust me alone in the house. At that time, she wasn't really a "dog person." I guess she was afraid I might do something bad so they left me in the back yard. It's a nice yard but a lot smaller than what I knew. They also had this thing called a fence. We don't have many of those on Cape Cod. It's made of metal and surrounds the yard so you can't get past it. I felt like I was trapped. I started digging a hole under the fence but started to wonder where I would go once I got out. After all, this was the city, and I have heard stories about the city and that made me nervous so I thought it best to try to get inside the house instead. I went to the back door and started scratching and scratching and scratching and scratching. Nothing happened. No matter how much I scratched there was just no getting in. I wasn't sure what else to do so I kept trying. I scratched so much my paws were raw. I finally decided to stop scratching because I thought it best to stay quiet and not attract a lot of attention.

The daytime wasn't too bad; I heard lots of kids playing and cars passing by, but at night the sounds of the city change. I tried to relax and sit quietly, but the city sounds are a lot different than noise at home, with lots of car horns, alarms, traffic, sirens, unfamiliar barks and voices in the distance. It all made me feel a bit nervous and unsettled, especially when it was getting dark out. It felt like they were never coming back. I wondered why they would leave me out there all alone. It was real scary.

I stayed close to the back door and curled up into a small ball. I heard sirens and then some coyotes started to howl! Finally, there was a familiar sound, and I instinctively joined in. I didn't know they were in the city too. This made me feel a little better. As things quieted down, I actually fell asleep. I was so tired. The stress was exhausting. I slept for a while and had a scary dream that ended nice. I dreamed I was being chased through the deserted city streets by a pack of wild coyotes. They didn't want me in their territory. I ran down this narrow dark alley, but at the end of the alley was the

60

light of the full moon shining on the ocean. The alley opened up to a beautiful sandy beach where the coyotes and I played and chased each other for fun. During our beach romp, I heard the surf but it was really a car pulling into the driveway and I woke up. It was them at last. They were home. I was so happy to see them, and they me until they got to the door. They looked at me and looked back at the splintered door. I had shredded it. Their mouths hung open. Mom and Dad kept apologizing to Grandma and Grandpa. Grandma looked angry but didn't say much. Grandpa said, "What are you going to do? It happens." Mom and Dad felt badly. Their dog ruined the door and they had neglected me to the point where I would do something so crazy! I know this because instead of getting the "bad dog" and lecture to follow, they hugged me and said they were sorry for leaving me in an unfamiliar place for so long. Honestly, what had they been thinking? After the initial shock of what I had done was over, they put together a plan that Dad would sand down and refinish the door. Then we all went to bed.

In the morning we had a nice breakfast together and then a beach walk. Yes there's even a beach in Boston! We go to Revere Beach, near Grandma and Grandpa's house. It's a really nice beach. It's the first public beach in the whole country! It's different from the Cape beaches because there's a busy street that runs along the side of it. But it's fun. There are lots of people rollerblading, running, and bike riding plus lots of restaurants for snacks. Grandma and Grandpa walk the beach almost every day and they move at a pretty good clip. They don't like to stop as much as I do, so I do my best to keep up.

After our beach walk, we head back to Grandma and Grandpa's. While Mom and Grandma finish cleaning up the breakfast dishes, Dad and Grandpa took the door off its hinges and put it into the back of Dad's truck while I supervised. As we headed out, we said our goodbyes. I don't think they were upset with me anymore because I got some nice pats, smiles, and even an invitation back!

62

Grandma said, "Shelby, you behave next time you come to my house!" so I was thrilled. I knew I was okay with that. What else could I possibly do to the house and why would I? I love my grandparents.

Shelby's Quick Trip to the Kettle Pond

Before our bed and breakfast guests come, they are told I live here. In fact, I think that's why most of them come! I'm certain I'm why most of our repeat customers keep coming back. I am great for business. I'm great company for our guests when Mom and Dad aren't home. People love to be greeted at the door by a cute red-coated dog wagging his bushy tail, especially after a long day at the beach.

Mom and Dad tell them all not to let me out if they're not home, but I always manage to get out. Someone always leaves the slider cracked just enough so I can let myself out. That usually sends the guests into a small panic but I never stay out for very long.

I usually make a quick trip up the street to the nice lady with the cat food; only now she gives me Milk Bones. Sometimes I stay out a bit longer if I decide to bury them in Mr. Carter's garden. I love the Carters. They are our neighbors from New Jersey, but they don't love me when I make holes in their garden. Anyway, I return home quickly so our guests don't get in trouble with Mom and Dad for letting me out. After all, I know what *that's* like. Some of them are careful not to let me out, but if I stand next to my leash by the door and cry or better yet bark, I am sure to get a quick walk. They usually take me to the pond or bike trail. Sometimes Mom and Dad have a hard time communicating with our guests because some don't speak any English. But I never have a hard time getting *my* point across. It seems everyone speaks dog! It took a while for Mom and

Dad to find out about the walks I was getting from our guests. It had been going on for years before they finally found out about it.

It happened one evening when Mom and Dad were going out for a nice dinner. Dad decided to take me to the beach before they left. I had my usual fun, then he dropped me off at home and they left. Just after they left, our guests from Germany came home. I did my usual "I'm so happy you've come home" routine and pranced around the house with excitement. Then I stood at the door and barked. Wolfgang, one of the Germen guests, quickly got my leash and took me out toward the pond.

On Cape Cod, there are as many ponds as there are days of the year: 365. Cape Cod is just 413 square miles. That's a lot of ponds in an area that is the same size as 10 Disney Worlds! That means in each Disney World there would more than 36 ponds in each. On Cape Cod we call them kettle ponds because they are in the shape of a kettle. Most were formed around 10,000 years ago when the glaciers retreated, and huge pieces of ice broke free from the larger glacier. The ice caps melted slowly where they came to rest and eventually formed our ponds. The one closest to my house, where Wolfgang and I headed to, is Great Pond. They call it Great Pond because of its size. I love going there. There are lily pads right along the shore with dragon flies and turtles resting. Both are fun to watch and if I am stealth-like, I can sneak up on them and observe. I try not to frighten them because I love their colors. Their iridescence catches my eye and I find it interesting since their shine is not something you see in fur. It's like nothing I have ever experienced before.

Unfortunately, no sooner did we turn down Great Pond Road, when who came cruising down the road in the truck but Mom and Dad. It seemed Mom forgot something and I was found out! Wolfgang explained how I barked and it seemed like I had been home alone for a long time, so he thought I needed a walk. They explained I had just been to the beach. Feeling the walk was a bit unnecessary, he turned around and took me back home. I hate when a good walk gets cut short!

Shelby and the Sharks

As you know, seals have always impressed me. I have always thought if there was any other animal I would like to be on Cape Cod, it would be a seal. They have a nice life here. They bask in the sun and enjoy their time on the beach. They frolic in the surf and make catching fish look fun. Life for them wasn't always so simple here. In fact, up until the late 1960s, there was a bounty on their heads. A fisherman would be paid five dollars for the nose of a seal. Fishermen believed the seals were eating all of "their" fish. Fortunately, in 1972 Congress enacted the Marine Mammal Protection Act and hunting seals was outlawed. Since they have been protected, the seals have come back and their numbers are strong. There are somewhere between 12,000 to 15,000 Grey Seals living on and around Cape Cod and the islands.

I often see seals on my beach walks. They see me, too. I see them stretch their necks up and bob up and down to watch me. They seem just as curious about me as I am about them. I even dream about them. Just the other morning, I woke myself up howling. I dreamed I was a seal swimming in the ocean with the humpback whales. The whales were singing their haunting songs and, as a seal, I started to join in. I started to sing in my dream and that's when I heard my howls and woke up.

More recently, I've been worried about the seals. It seems Cape Cod isn't as safe for them as it once was. People aren't the only problems for the seals; sharks are too. Seals and sharks have always had their issues but the real trouble started in 2009 when six Great White Sharks were spotted feeding on seals just off Light House Beach in Chatham. The local shark expert and his crew tagged five of them to learn more about their habits. Up until then, we had no idea where these sharks went. It turns out, some are wintering in deep water off of Jacksonville, Florida, but why? This may seem like a tough question for most, but not for our local whale biologists. The assumption is they are feeding on Right Whale calves. I know this is an unpleasant idea for most people who love whales. The thought of a baby whale being eaten by a nasty shark is quite unsettling, especially baby Right Whales because they are the most endangered of all the great whales.

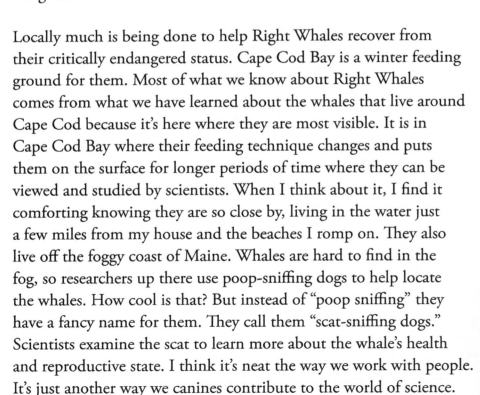

Locally much is being done to help Right Whales recover from their critically endangered status. Cape Cod Bay is a winter feeding ground for them. Most of what we know about Right Whales comes from what we have learned about the whales that live around Cape Cod because it's here where they are most visible. It is in Cape Cod Bay where their feeding technique changes and puts them on the surface for longer periods of time where they can be viewed and studied by scientists. When I think about it, I find it comforting knowing they are so close by, living in the water just a few miles from my house and the beaches I romp on. They also live off the foggy coast of Maine. Whales are hard to find in the fog, so researchers up there use poop-sniffing dogs to help locate the whales. How cool is that? But instead of "poop sniffing" they have a fancy name for them. They call them "scat-sniffing dogs." Scientists examine the scat to learn more about the whale's health and reproductive state. I think it's neat the way we work with people. It's just another way we canines contribute to the world of science.

The big question about the sharks and seals in 2010 was, would the Great Whites return to their abundant food supply around Cape Cod? As the experts predicted, they did, all summer long and in big numbers. The beaches in Chatham and Orleans were closed to swimming on and off throughout the season. People witnessed seal attacks off Truro and Provincetown and even my hometown of Eastham. Whale watch boats were seeing the sharks and people loved it. Tee shirt sales rose. Our guests came home with shirts that say, "I swam with the sharks of Chatham" and "Let's do lunch!"

It's all pretty exciting, but I keep thinking, "What about the seals?" How do they live with this threat every day? Do they even know the threat exists? It all gets me thinking about myself. I hunt squirrels and rabbits because "that's what dogs do," and I think nothing of it. But what does that make me, some ferocious animal with killer instincts? Am I like a shark plucking innocent seals off the beach, like pulling petals off a flower? Am I worse than a shark? After all, the shark needs the seals to survive. I don't need the squirrels. Mom and Dad feed me great food. It all comes down to instinct. I guess, as animals we are all the same, following some ingrained path, dogs chasing rabbits, seals chasing fish. But it just doesn't feel the same as sharks killing seals. Fortunately, we dogs and seals have our great looks. The sharks don't. Their ferocious teeth make them appear mean and nasty. Is it right to judge them so differently? I think not. They are just doing what they were meant to do. Just as I see that the neighborhood doesn't get overrun by squirrels, the sharks keep the balance of nature in the ocean. If they didn't, might the people resort to hunting the seals again? I'd rather let the sharks take care of things.

Shelby's Summer Season Ends

Seeing the summer come to an end is sometimes a difficult time in our home especially for Mom and Dad. It means back to school for them and fewer and fewer guests. We take fewer day trips and whale watches and excursions. Our busy summer pace slows, but sometimes we need that. The summer humidity drops off and the cool dry September air is invigorating yet calming to my soul. The beach plums ripen. Mom says the color of the marsh changes from its summer green to "Shelby Red." I am perfectly camouflaged among the sand, the golden rod and the fading marsh grasses. I no longer stand out and I am ready. My summer life is filled with entertainment and often I am the entertainer. Even though I love my summer lifestyle, I am ready for the change of pace. The change is good. It is healthy and makes me appreciate the summer fun when it comes my way again.

That's not to say the winters on Cape Cod aren't fun; they are, but the pace is much slower. The cold, the snow, the ice—it's all beautiful but in a different way. Our life feels different, calmer. We tend to relax more, snuggle more and on the real cold nights I even let the cat join us in bed. Some winters are so cold the water in Cape Cod Bay freezes over. It looks like the frozen tundra and I pretend to be a wolf or a white arctic fox searching for food as I traverse the frozen ice fields. The nor'easters blow in, the beaches erode. The island ferries are canceled. At times, I find life in the winter a bit more interesting because it's less predictable than the summer. The winters seem harder on Mom and Dad and they seem to crave the warmth of the summer sun more so than I do. For me, the change is easy because it's a not a complete change. The two biggest constants are always by my side, Mom and Dad. Together with them, I will always look forward to another day, summer *or* winter, and my adventurous life as a Cape Cod Dog.

Acknowledgements

This story took a dog's lifetime to write and a lot of encouragement from a great deal of people that Shelby and I hold dear. Most of the encouragement came from my family. Thank you Mom and Dad for raising me to believe I could do anything I set my mind to. That's what gave me the nerve to even consider taking on this project. Mom, if it was up to me, this would still be on a hand-written legal pad. Thanks for your energy, time and quick fingers. Dad, I know you miss your special walks with Shelby, and yes, you were right: he kept all your secrets. I know nothing. Also, we are truly sorry about the door, the chair, and (last but not least) the brand-new couch.

To my dear sister Donna, where do I begin? Thank you for your personal and professional advice and guidance, and unending patience. After long phone calls full of questions, I finally let you hang up only to call you right back with just one more "quick question." Your answers were never quick. They were well thought out and explained, and often you continued to think about them days after I had moved on. Thanks for trying to help me get it right. This story would not be as it is today without all this thoughtfulness and your sharp eyes.

To Judy for always being there when we couldn't be. For picking up where we left off in his life and making it complete.

To Jenny, for bringing Shelby to life again with your beautiful illustrations.

To Bob, for your help recounting all the exciting times we had with Shelby. It was fun to remember them all, and decide which was "book worthy." Both you and Shelby have been my biggest inspiration. You've been my sounding board, my editor, my idea guy, and our playmate. All these adventures have been with you. I can not think of anyone I would have rather have had them with. I know *you* were his best friend and I'm okay with that.

Most of my thanks must go to Shelby, who showed us 16 years of unconditional love that made our lives whole. Thank you for allowing us to share in your escapades and adventures. Chesney has some big paws to fill. You will never be replaced. We will miss and love you always.

Nancy Scaglione-Peck is a high school science teacher on Cape Cod and a naturalist for the Dolphin Fleet Whale Watch in Provincetown. She was a marine mammal trainer at Mystic Aquarium in Mystic, Connecticut, and worked as a naturalist for the Provincetown Center for Coastal Studies. She and her husband, Bob, operate The Outer Cape Escape Bed and Breakfast in Eastham, Massachusetts, where they have lived for more than 20 years. They share their home with their Golden Retriever, Chesney.

Jenny Kelley holds a BFA in painting from the Rhode Island School of Design. An award-winning artist (and dog lover), she has been featured in Cape Cod Life and Cape Cod Magazine, and is a member of the Copley Society of Art in Boston. This is Jenny's eighth illustrated book. She also enjoys being a high school art teacher. To see more of her artwork, visit www.jennykelley.com